E
MC

McCully, Emily
Arnold

Speak up, Blanche!

$14.89

SPEAK UP, BLANCHE!

For Jolly and Alfred

Speak Up, Blanche!
Copyright © 1991 by Emily Arnold McCully
Printed in the U.S.A. All rights reserved.
1 2 3 4 5 6 7 8 9 10
First Edition

Library of Congress Cataloging-in-Publication Data

McCully, Emily Arnold.
Speak up, Blanche! / Emily Arnold McCully.
    p.   cm.
    Summary: Stagestruck Blanche would like to be a part of a
theatrical bear troupe's new play, but her shyness causes problems
until she discovers a special talent of her very own.
    ISBN 0-06-024227-2. — ISBN 0-06-024228-0 (lib. bdg.)
    [1. Theater—Fiction. 2. Bashfulness—Fiction. 3. Artists—
Fiction. 4. Bears—Fiction.] I. Title.
PZ7.M478415Sp 1991   90-36945
[E]—dc20   CIP
                                                            AC

SPEAK UP, BLANCHE!

FARM THEATER →

The Strange Pudding
Opens

Emily Arnold McCully

HarperCollins*Publishers*

At the Farm Theater, Bruno, Sophie, Zaza, Sarah, and Edwin were having a barbecue to celebrate the final performance of their latest hit, *The Evil Spell*. The very next day they would begin rehearsing Bruno's new play, *The Strange Pudding*.

"Look, someone's coming," said Sarah, "...in a snazzy car."

"Why, it's Eva!" cried Sophie. "She used to be an actress long ago. When we turned the farm into a theater, she was such a help!"

"Welcome, dear Eva," said Bruno. "What brings you here?"

"I have a favor to ask of you," said Eva.

"Of course!" cried Bruno. He would never forget that Eva had given them their curtain and box seats.

"I have a young grandchild called Blanche," explained Eva. "I think she is stagestruck. May she come here for a while and learn the craft of acting?"

"We would be honored," said Bruno.

"How delightful, how kind," said Eva. "As it happens, Blanche is with me, in the car. She is a little shy."

"Oh, brother," said Zaza to Sarah. "And she wants to act?"

"Come, Blanche," coaxed Eva. "Come say hello."

"ʜᴇʟʟᴏ," said Blanche.

"What did she say?" asked Zaza.

"She said, 'Hello,'" said Eva. "Speak up, Blanche, dear."

Blanche took a deep breath, opened her mouth wide, and said, "ʜᴇʟʟᴏ." She was an only child and was used to spending most of her time alone. She wanted to tell everyone how much she loved the theater, but the words would not come out.

"What are you carrying?" asked Edwin.

Blanche blushed. "JUST MY SKETCHBOOK," she said.

"Perhaps Zaza could work with Blanche," Sophie said. "She can be an excellent teacher when she puts her mind to it."

Zaza was not thrilled, but she agreed.

"May I look at your sketches?" Edwin whispered to Blanche. She shook her head. "She *is* very shy," Edwin thought.

The next day, the family rehearsed *The Strange Pudding* and Blanche watched. She loved the way Zaza screamed when the pudding jiggled and the way Edwin jumped when it spilled.

Then Zaza said, "Come on, Blanche, it's time for your acting lesson. We can perform a scene from the play."

Blanche's legs began to shake.

"Take a deep breath," said Zaza. "It's natural to feel nervous at first."
Zaza handed her a script. "You are Lackadaisica, the maid. I am the
duchess. You have served me a strange pudding.

"*Lackadaisica!*" said Zaza in a loud, bossy voice. "Please explain the meaning of this strange pudding!"

Blanche stared at Zaza.

"Blanche! It's your turn to say your line now," said Zaza in her regular voice.

"IT IS A PERFECTLY NORMAL PUDDING," read Blanche.

"Oh, dear," said Zaza. She explained that actors must speak so that the audience can hear. In this scene, the actor must show that the maid is angry when the duchess calls her pudding strange. They tried again. Blanche continued to shake and speak in a tiny whisper.

"For heaven's sake, Blanche!" Zaza said. She stormed off the stage.

Blanche opened her sketchbook. A quick drawing always helped when she felt bad.

Outside, Sarah was sawing boards for the duchess's bed.

"That Blanche is hopeless!" Zaza told her.

"What a shame," said Sarah. "She is so nice."

"Well, I don't think she has any talent," said Zaza.

"*I* will try teaching her!" said Sarah.

Blanche felt terrible. She tried to be brave.

When Sarah came in to give her another lesson, Blanche was ready to try again.

"Let's pretend that you are the duchess in the play," Sarah began. "I will be the maid, and I will serve you the strange pudding."

"ₒₖₐᵧ," said Blanche.

"Take a bite," said Sarah.

Blanche pretended to take a bite of the pudding.

"You are not *acting*," said Sarah. "Show us how it tastes." Blanche took another bite.

"Show us your *feelings*!" cried Sarah. "Watch how I do it." Sarah took a bite of pudding. "*Blaaaaaaaaaaahhhhhhhhhhp*! See? Now the audience knows the pudding is strange."

Blanche tried to do what Sarah had done. But she felt much too embarrassed.

Bruno whispered, "I'm afraid Blanche will never be an actress."

"I know," said Sophie. "Some people just don't belong on the stage."

Bruno was worried. "What will we tell Eva?"

"Maybe she needs a little more time," said Sophie.

"She has *had* time," said Zaza. "She stinks!"

"It's true," said Sarah.

Blanche looked out at the family, and she could see that they had all given up on her. She wanted more than anything in the world to be part of this lively group, but they didn't want her at all! She ran out of the theater to find a place where she could be alone.

The ticket booth was perfect. She sat on a little chair, out of sight.

Suddenly an unfamiliar voice boomed over her head.

"Excuse me, Miss. I need tickets for opening night!"

Blanche was startled out of her wits.

"<small>HOW MANY</small>?" she said at last.

"Speak up!" bellowed the stranger. "I can't hear you!"

Blanche was so flustered that she upset the box of tickets.

"What's going on?" said Sarah.

"First she can't act," grumbled Zaza. "Then she can't sell tickets."

"What *can* she do?" said Sarah.

"Everyone is good at something!" said Sophie.

"*I* know!" cried Edwin. "She can collect props for me!"

"PROPS?" asked Blanche.

"Things the actors need for the play," Edwin explained. They told Blanche to go next door and borrow a rocking horse, a washtub, and a tuba.

"ALL RIGHT," said Blanche.

The countryside was perfectly beautiful! On another day she'd have drawn a picture of it. But now she had an important job! She came to a house and raised her hand to knock, but she just couldn't do it. Then the door flew open.

"I thought someone was there," said a voice. "Are you lost?"

Blanche took a deep breath and blurted, "I want a rocking horse, a washtub, and a tuba."

There was a pause and then the voice replied, "If this is a practical joke, child, it isn't funny!" The door shut in Blanche's face.

Blanche was completely miserable. If anything else went wrong she didn't think she could bear it! Now she would have to admit that she had failed at props, too.

She wandered backstage until she heard voices. When she walked into the room, she heard Zaza say, "Uh oh."

The family was painting sets for the new play. Nothing looked real, and there was lots of spilled paint.

"Blanche, dear," said Sophie. "Where are the props?"

"Your neighbor didn't know who I was," said Blanche. "She thought it was a joke."

"Oh, brother," said Zaza to Sarah. "She is utterly useless!"

"Excuse me," said Blanche. "You know, I'm sure I could paint good sets for you. Then you could spend your time rehearsing."

Bruno said, "Blanche, we are all very sorry. But it has not worked out, having you at the theater...."

"We are sending you back home, dear," said Sophie.

Blanche stared at them. Then, inside her, something exploded.

"JUST A MINUTE!" she shouted. "YOU WANT ME TO SHOW MY FEELINGS? WELL, HERE THEY ARE! I FEEL BAD WHEN I CAN'T LEARN TO ACT! I FEEL BAD WHEN I SPILL THE TICKETS! I FEEL BAD WHEN I CAN'T BORROW PROPS FROM STRANGERS! BUT YOU AREN'T FAIR! I DRAW AND PAINT VERY WELL! I CAN MAKE WONDERFUL SETS FOR YOUR PLAY!"

"My, my," Sophie said at last.

"Wow, Blanche," Zaza said. "What a great performance!"

"If only you could do that on stage," said Bruno.

"You're right," said Sophie. "We were not fair to you."

"I think we should let her try painting the sets," said Edwin.

"I do too," said Sarah.

"Well, *we* are certainly lousy at set painting," said Zaza.

So Blanche tried her hand at the sets. She had never painted such big pictures before. First she made little sketches in her book.

Then she copied them onto huge flats.

Days later, when she had finished, she was very pleased.

The family was amazed.

"These are masterpieces!" Bruno declared. "At last, our plays will have the scenery they deserve!"

"What a talent you have," said Edwin.

"Wow, Blanche!" Zaza said again. They sang "For She's a Jolly Good Fellow!" and pulled Blanche into a dance.

Even Eva forgot her disappointment that Blanche would not be a great actress at the Farm Theater.

"You never told me you could paint like this!" she said.

"I wasn't sure I could, myself," said Blanche.

"And, by the way, you are no longer shy," Eva observed.

"No," said Blanche. "I am an artist."